Lili on Stage

Rachel Isadora

PaperStar

The Putnam & Grosset Group

To my father

Copyright © 1995 by Rachel Isadora
All rights reserved. This book, or parts thereof, may not be
reproduced in any form without permission in writing from the publisher.
A PaperStar Book, published in 1998 by The Putnam & Grosset Group,
200 Madison Avenue, New York, NY 10016. PaperStar is a registered
trademark of The Putnam Berkley Group, Inc. The PaperStar logo
is a trademark of The Putnam Berkley Group, Inc.
Originally published in 1995 by G. P. Putnam's Sons.
Published simultaneously in Canada
Printed in the United States of America
Hand-lettering by David Gatti
Text set in Goudy Oldstyle
Library of Congress Cataloging-in-Publication Data
Isadora, Rachel. Lili on stage / Rachel Isadora. p. cm.
Summary: Lili is thrilled to be dancing the part of a guest
in the party scene of The Nutcracker ballet.
[1. Ballet—Fiction. 2. Nutcracker (Ballet)—Fiction.] I. Title.
PZ7.1763Lk 1995 [E]—dc20 94-5982 CIP AC
ISBN 0-698-11651-8
1 3 5 7 9 10 8 6 4 2

Note to the Reader

The Nutcracker is a story set in Germany many years ago. One Christmas Eve, Marie's family hosts the evening's celebration. Herr Drosselmeyer, Marie's godfather, gives her a nutcracker. Marie's brother, Fritz, is jealous, and he grabs the nutcracker from her arms and breaks it. Drosselmeyer repairs the nutcracker, and the splendid party continues. That night, Marie falls asleep by the Christmas tree, holding the nutcracker close to her.

When Marie awakes suddenly, she finds herself surrounded by giant, evil mice. The nutcracker, no longer wooden but alive, comes to her rescue, leading a troop of soldiers into a battle against the mice. Once the battle is won, and the King mouse slain, the brave nutcracker turns into a prince. Placing a crown on Marie's head, he leads her to his Kingdom of Sweets. There she meets the Sugar Plum Fairy, Hot Chocolate, Marzipan, Dew Drop, Tea, Mother Ginger, Polschinelle, and many others. They welcome her with their different dances.

For Marie, it is magic. Afterward, she and the Prince fly into the night sky and continue their journey through the Kingdom of Sweets.

Rachel Isadora

It is opening night of *The Nutcracker* ballet. Lili has seen the ballet performed before, but tonight she'll be on stage as a guest in the party scene.

Lili arrives at the theater. She talks with Nanette and Kathy backstage while everyone waits to go into the studio to warm up.

Cindi writes in her diary.

Donna stretches.

Jina limbers up.

Some of the girls play jacks while they wait.

Patrick catches up on his homework.

Lili changes into practice clothes and goes into the studio. While warming up, everyone thinks about what Marina, the ballet mistress, told them in rehearsals:

No speaking on stage.

Hold your head high so even the people in the last row can see your face.

Don't let your attention wander.
You are an important part
of the ballet.

Never count
the beats
out loud.

Don't scratch your nose.
The audience sees
everything.

Marina wants to rehearse the party scene from the first act. "Find your partners, please," she says. After many weeks of rehearsal, everyone knows their part by heart.

"Half hour to curtain!" the stage manager announces over the intercom. Lili and her friends hurry to the makeup room.

"Your lipstick shade is too light, Meg," Marina says. "On stage

we use darker shades or the audience will not see your mouth!"

"Too much mascara and liner," Marina tells Gillian. "Your eyes will look like black holes from the audience."

When everyone is made up, Marina takes them to the costume room. She introduces them to Margaret, the wardrobe mistress.
Margaret helps Lili fasten her dress.

"Remember, you may not eat or sit once you are in your costume," Margaret tells everyone.

"Five minutes to curtain!" the stage manager announces.

Marina takes the children to the stage.

They wait in the wings. Lili stands with
Nanette.

"I'm nervous," Nanette says.

"Me, too," Lili says. "Remember, we're going
to a party," she tells Nanette, and they both
giggle.

It's time to go on. Suddenly all the rehearsals fade away, and Lili
feels as if the party is real. She watches Herr Drosselmeyer present
the nutcracker with a flourish, and she almost believes he is magic.

After she exits, Lili watches from behind the curtain as the Prince leads Marie away to his Kingdom of Sweets.

Act I ends and Lili and her friends take their bows. The audience applauds and shouts, "Bravo! Bravo!"

On the way to the changing room, Lili sees
the dancers who will perform in Act II:

Marzipan

Hot Chocolate

Tea

Dew Drop

Lili hopes to dance the role of Polschinelle next year.

Waltz of the Flowers

Sugar Plum Fairy
and her Cavalier

Candycane

Marie and the Prince

Arabian

Mother Ginger and Polschinelle

Before the curtain goes up for Act II, Lili takes flowers to her favorite ballerina.

"These will bring me good luck," says Gabrielle, smiling. She signs a toe shoe and gives it to Lili.

"From one ballerina to another!" Lili reads.

When Lili gets home, she is too excited to go to sleep. Tomorrow night there will be another performance, and the magic will begin again. . . .